FARMERS MARKET SURPRISE!

Thank you to all the farmers and artisans
who grow and create wonderful things. – HM

First Edition 2018
Kane Miller, A Division of EDC Publishing

For information contact:
Kane Miller, A Division of EDC Publishing
www.kanemiller.com
www.edcpub.com
www.usbornebooksandmore.com

Library of Congress Control Number: 2017958230

Manufactured by Regent Publishing Services, Hong Kong
Printed March 2018 in ShenZhen, Guangdong, China
1 2 3 4 5 6 7 8 9 10

ISBN: 978-1-61067-748-6

FARMERS MARKET SURPRISE!

by Hazel Mitchell

Kane Miller
A DIVISION OF EDC PUBLISHING

COUNT & SEARCH

On Saturday morning, Alice and Addy went to the farmers market.

"Everything at the market is so fresh," said Alice.
"And yummy!" said Addy.

"Look, Alice," said Addy, "fresh honey!"

"Yum," said Addy, "I love cheese! Let's buy some."

"Mmmmm! Ice cream," said Addy.
"Oh! Choco Fudge, my favorite," said Alice.

"Ah," said Addy. "I love the smell of freshly baked bread!"

"What pretty handmade paper," said Alice.
"Let's choose some!" said Addy.

"Ripe berries," said Addy.
"Fresh from the fields," said Alice.

6

We will buy **SIX** boxes of berries.

"Oh, smell those lemons, Alice," said Addy.
"Lemonade!" said Alice.

"We need more candles," said Addy.
"We do?" said Alice.

"Alice, look! Cupcakes!" said Addy.
"Addy, I don't think I can carry anything else," said Alice.

"Do we really need ten cupcakes?" said Alice.
"Oh, yes!" said Addy.

"My feet hurt," said Alice.
"We're almost home. You can sit in the garden and rest," said Addy.

Alice sipped her tea.
I wonder if Addy forgot, she thought.

Meanwhile, inside ...

Cat made cheese
sandwiches.

Pig and Raccoon
made cards.

Toucan prepared
ice cream sundaes
with berries.

The Panda twins squeezed lemons for lemonade and added honey.

Giraffe arranged the sunflowers.

And Addy put the candles on the cupcakes ... and called Alice to come inside.

How many can you find?

Search the pictures for at least ...

 **10 Butterflies**

 **7 Frogs**

6 Birds

5 Dogs